STAR CROSSED MIRACLE IN THE MOUNTAINS

Spines

Star Crossed Miracle in the Mountains

Philip Tate

Chapter 1

Foundations of a Scholar

Wake Forest College stood as a sanctuary for seekers of wisdom and faith, its stately oaks bearing witness to generations of aspirants. In 1878, a bright-eyed young man named William Scott McBannon arrived, and so this story begins. He was eager to embrace both the divine and the natural mysteries of the world. Known simply as Bill, he hailed from the lowlands near Laurinburg, where his early years were steeped in the lessons of his strict but loving aunt.

Bill's life began under a sky laden with omens. The night of his birth in 1859 was marked by a meteor shower that lit up the heavens, an event that villagers whispered foretold an extraordinary destiny. Born into a family of modest farmers, his early days were spent in a house surrounded by fields and the thick embrace of the lowland woods. Even as a boy, Bill exhibited an insatiable curiosity. He would wander along streams, turning over rocks and pressing leaves into the pages of a small journal his father had given him. His mother often found him sitting under the old pecan tree, lost in thought as if the very wind carried whispers of mysteries waiting to be unraveled.

His aunt, Margaret McBannon—whom he affectionately called Aunt Maggie—became the cornerstone of his education. A woman of formidable presence, Margaret was tall and slender, with silver-threaded auburn hair often pinned into a neat bun. Her piercing blue eyes seemed to see straight through a person, and her voice, though warm, carried the weight of authority. Margaret had studied in Edinburgh, and she returned to Laurinburg with a sharp mind and an insistence on excellence that she passed on to her nephew. She believed that discipline and wonder could coexist, and she wove together teachings on scripture and science, history and nature. Bill often remembered her favorite saying: "God reveals Himself in both the written Word and the unwritten wonders of this earth."

Bill himself was a curious blend of his upbringing. Slightly built but wiry, he had a mop of dark hair that fell into his sharp blue eyes when he was deep in thought. His quiet demeanor belied an intense curiosity and a penchant for observation. Often found sketching plants or scribbling notes, he seemed to carry an unspoken conviction that every detail of the world was worth recording. By the time he reached adolescence, Bill's intellect and curiosity had become undeniable. Aunt Maggie's firm guidance ensured he was prepared for the academic rigor ahead, and he left home with her blessing and her parting words echoing in his ears: "Remember, Bill, the world will always have its questions— find the answers that matter."

At nineteen, Bill arrived at Wake Forest College. The

transition from his quiet upbringing to the bustling life of academia was overwhelming. Yet, there was something about the campus that felt almost sacred. The stately oaks that framed the grounds seemed to welcome him as an old friend, and the chapel's bell tolled like a call to purpose. Here, Bill's boundless curiosity found fertile ground. He quickly immersed himself in studies that balanced theology with the natural sciences, navigating the delicate interplay between faith and reason with an ease that surprised even his professors.

Though life at college was demanding, Bill thrived. He spent long hours in the library, his fingers tracing lines of scripture and scientific diagrams with equal reverence. He became known among his peers for his quiet intensity and his habit of carrying a leather-bound notebook wherever he went, jotting down ideas, sketches, and observations. To him, every leaf, every stone, every lesson was a fragment of a larger truth—a truth he felt called to uncover.

CHAPTER 2

A PATH UNFOLDS

As Bill matured, so too did his academic ambitions. He had always been deeply enamored of the gifts the world had to offer, and so he followed his heart. At the University of North Carolina, where he pursued graduate studies in geology and botany, he discovered a profound allure in the mysteries of the natural world. What began as a curiosity evolved into an insatiable drive to uncover the stories hidden within the land. Surveying work during weekends brought him face-to-face with the rugged beauty of the forested hills, but it was the scattered quartz stones that captivated him most.

University life at the University of North Carolina expanded Bill's horizons. While he excelled in both geology and botany, it was the fieldwork that stirred something profound within him. On one particular survey trip into the foothills, Bill encountered the scattered quartz stones that would become a lifelong obsession.

The late afternoon sun painted the forest in golden hues

as Bill adjusted the strap of his surveyor's bag and set down his tools. The ground beneath his feet was uneven, dotted with stones that gleamed like fractured mirrors in the fading light. He crouched down and picked one up, turning it over in his hands. The quartz was smooth and cool, its edges catching the light and refracting it into fleeting rainbows. But what fascinated him most was its presence here, in this forest, so far from where it might have formed.

These were no ordinary rocks. Each one seemed to hold a story, its surface marked by the passage of time and the violence of its creation. Bill imagined ancient forces at work, deep within the earth—pressures so immense they birthed these crystalline fragments and hurled them skyward in some primordial explosion. He envisioned the stones raining down, settling into the soil like seeds of a forgotten past. The thought sent a shiver down his spine.

"It's as if the earth remembers," he murmured to himself, his voice almost reverent.

His colleagues teased him for his fascination, but Bill didn't mind. To him, the quartz was a puzzle, a relic of the earth's turbulent history. He began collecting them, stuffing his bag until it was nearly too heavy to carry. That evening, back in his rented room near campus, he spread the stones out on his desk and examined them by lamplight. Their translucent beauty seemed almost otherworldly, and he couldn't shake the feeling that they held answers to questions he had yet to ask.

Botany, too, held a magnetic pull. During another excursion, Bill discovered a cluster of rare wildflowers thriving on a rocky slope. The delicate blossoms seemed to defy the harsh conditions, their vibrant colors a testament to resilience. Kneeling to examine them, he marveled at how life found a way to flourish in even the most unforgiving environments. Each leaf and petal seemed to whisper a story of survival and symbiosis, reinforcing his belief that the natural world held profound lessons for humanity.

One evening, Bill returned to his room with a small collection of specimens. By lamplight, he meticulously sketched their details, noting their textures and colors. His journals became tomes of discovery, filled with diagrams and musings that blurred the line between science and faith. To Bill, every plant and stone was a fragment of a grander design, each revealing a facet of the Creator's ingenuity.

His professors began to notice his singular focus and encouraged him to pursue his studies further.

"You have a gift for seeing the unseen," one mentor remarked.

"The stones and leaves speak to you in a way few can understand."

He also remembered his aunt in every glimpse of fascination, for she had instilled in him a love of books and a thirst for curiosity.

Bill's days became a blend of study and exploration. The forests around the university became his sanctuary, a place where he could lose himself in the mysteries of creation. Yet, despite his dedication, he often felt as though he was on the cusp of something greater—an elusive truth that lay just beyond his grasp.

CHAPTER 3

BILL MEETS JANE

The library at Wake Forest was Bill's sanctuary. Its towering shelves filled with books, the scent of aged paper, and the hushed whispers of students created an atmosphere of quiet reverence. One late afternoon, as sunlight filtered through the tall windows and cast golden streaks across the polished floors, Bill found himself engrossed in a text on geological formations.

The sound of firm footsteps broke his concentration. He glanced up just as a woman appeared at the end of the aisle, her presence commanding despite her delicate frame. Jane Wishart Lindley, the librarian, was a vision of composure and quiet strength. Her chestnut hair was swept into an elegant bun, and loose tendrils framed her face, softening her angular jawline. Her hazel eyes, flecked with gold, held an intensity that seemed to draw the world into focus. She wore a simple dress of deep blue, its cut practical but flattering, and a thin silver chain rested at her collarbone, glinting in the fading light.

Jane's gaze landed on Bill's growing stack of books, scattered haphazardly across the table. Clearing her throat gently, she approached. "Mr. McBannon, I presume?" Her voice was calm, measured, yet carried a hint of amusement.

Bill blinked, momentarily caught off guard. "Yes, ma'am. I'm Bill. How—how can I help you?"

Her lips curved into a small smile. "I believe the question is how I might help you. The library has its rules, and your desk appears to be testing their limits."

Bill glanced at the books, a faint flush rising to his cheeks. "I'm sorry—I didn't realize. I was a bit... carried away."

Jane's smile widened slightly. "So I see. Geological formations?"

Bill nodded, feeling both embarrassed and intrigued. "Yes. I was studying quartz deposits and their origins. They seem to tell stories, don't they? Stories of the earth's memory."

Her expression softened, curiosity sparking in her hazel eyes. "The earth's memory. That's a poetic way to put it."

As she helped him tidy up, their conversation deepened. Jane revealed her own love for literature and science, her voice tinged with a passion that mirrored his own. Bill found himself drawn not just to her knowledge, but to the way she moved and spoke, her every gesture precise yet unhurried, as though she had all the time in the world to listen and understand.

By the time the sun dipped below the horizon, casting the library in a warm, amber glow, Bill realized something had shifted. Jane wasn't just another librarian or a passing acquaintance. She was someone who, like the quartz stones and wildflowers, seemed to hold a story worth discovering.

CHAPTER 4

BENEATH THE LIBRARY'S GLOW

The days following Bill's first meeting with Jane were marked by an inexplicable pull toward the library, as if the quiet halls held more than just books—they held the promise of discovery, of conversations that lingered in the mind long after they ended. Bill, always drawn to the solitude of his studies, found himself increasingly aware of Jane's presence. She carried herself with a quiet grace, her hands moving deftly over the spines of books as she cataloged them, her hazel eyes sharp with curiosity and understanding.

Their encounters at first were brief, often marked by a polite exchange as Jane moved about her duties and Bill pored over his studies. Yet, there was something unspoken between them, an undercurrent of intrigue that neither fully acknowledged nor resisted. It was in the way Bill would glance up from his notes just as Jane passed by, in the way her lips curved slightly whenever she noticed him lost in thought.

One evening, as autumn's crisp air whispered through the stone corridors of Wake Forest, Bill lingered in the library later than usual. The oil lamps cast flickering shadows along the bookshelves, and Jane, as was her routine, was making her final rounds before closing.

"Still lost in the mysteries of quartz?" Jane's voice broke the quiet, her tone carrying a gentle amusement.

Bill looked up, momentarily disoriented before offering a sheepish smile. "It seems I can't stop wondering about them. They hold history in their depths. I find myself wanting to read their past, to understand where they came from."

Jane stepped closer, her curiosity evident. "And what have they told you so far?"

Bill hesitated, sensing that her question carried weight beyond idle conversation. He ran a hand over his leather-bound notebook, then met her gaze. "That nothing is random. Everything is placed where it is for a reason, whether by nature's force or something greater."

Jane studied him for a moment, then nodded. "That's a rather poetic way to look at geology."

Bill chuckled. "Science and poetry aren't as separate as we like to think. I suspect you know that better than most."

A pause stretched between them, but it was not uncomfortable. Instead, it carried the weight of something unspoken, something waiting to be understood. Then Jane reached over and pulled a book from the shelf beside him, its spine worn from years of handling.

"This is one of my favorites," she said, handing it to him. "The Natural Philosophy of the Universe. It's a study on the patterns that connect everything in nature, from the movement of the stars to the structure of plants."

Bill turned the book over in his hands, noting the delicate care with which it had been preserved. "You think I'll like it?"

"I think you'll see yourself in it."

Their conversations deepened with each passing week. What began as discussions about geology and literature turned into late-night musings on faith, purpose, and the unknown. Jane's love for literature matched Bill's love for discovery, and soon their words intertwined like vines growing toward the same light.

One evening, as the rain drummed softly against the stained-glass windows, Bill found Jane sitting at a table near the library's grand window, lost in thought. She looked up as he approached, a warm smile gracing her features.

"I was beginning to think you'd abandoned your studies for the night," she teased.

Bill set his books down beside hers. "Not entirely. But I think I've found something even more compelling than quartz formations."

Jane raised a curious brow. "And what might that be?"

Bill hesitated for only a moment before answering. "The way people are drawn to certain places, certain books, certain —" he met her gaze, "—certain people."

A flicker of something unreadable passed through Jane's expression, but she did not look away. Instead, she reached for the book she had been reading and turned it toward him. "Do you know what this is?"

Bill glanced at the cover. "The Odyssey."

Jane nodded. "It's about journeys—ones we choose and ones that choose us."

A quiet understanding passed between them. There was

something unfolding, something neither of them had planned, but neither wished to stop.

As the months wore on, their bond deepened. Walks through the campus gardens became frequent, their discussions weaving seamlessly between scholarly pursuits and the uncharted territory of personal dreams. Bill spoke of the cabin he hoped to build one day, a retreat high in the mountains where he could study and observe the stars. Jane shared her love for the written word, her dreams of preserving knowledge and creating a space where minds could come alive.

One crisp winter evening, as snowflakes drifted lazily onto the stone steps of the library, Bill hesitated before saying goodbye. Jane stood in the doorway, wrapped in her shawl, her cheeks tinged with the cold.

"Jane," he said, his voice steady despite the way his heart quickened, "if I were to ask if I might call on you outside of these library walls, would you say yes?"

She studied him for a long moment before answering, a slow smile spreading across her lips. "Yes, Bill. I believe I would."

CHAPTER 5

A LOVE WRITTEN IN THE STARS

The winter months passed in a quiet, gentle rhythm, marked by late-night walks beneath Wake Forest's towering oaks and hushed conversations that grew softer, more intimate with time. Bill and Jane's courtship was not one of grand gestures, but of steady devotion, built through shared books, long discussions, and unspoken understandings. There was a certainty in their love, a feeling that had been present from their very first conversation in the library.

One evening, as the first hints of spring awakened the earth, Bill and Jane sat side by side on a wooden bench overlooking the campus gardens. The scent of magnolia blossoms filled the air, and the faint glow of the gas lamps cast a golden hue on Jane's features. Bill turned to her, his voice steady but laced with emotion.

"Jane, I have spent my life seeking answers in the patterns of the earth and sky. But you... you are the one thing I cannot explain, and I don't wish to. I only know that my days are better when they begin and end with you."

Jane smiled, the soft candlelight reflecting in her hazel eyes. "Bill," she whispered, her voice barely more than a breath, "I believe we were meant to find each other."

He took her hands in his, calloused from years of exploration yet infinitely gentle as he held hers. "Will you be my wife?"

A moment stretched between them, filled with the rustling of leaves and the distant hum of laughter from students passing by. Then, with the quiet certainty that had always defined them, Jane nodded. "Yes, Bill. I will."

Their wedding was a modest affair, held in a small chapel near the college. The pews were filled with close friends, professors, and a few townsfolk who had come to admire the couple's quiet devotion. Bill's Aunt Maggie arrived from Laurinburg, her sharp eyes soft with pride as she watched the nephew she had raised step forward to meet his bride.

As Jane walked down the aisle, dressed in an elegant yet simple gown of ivory lace, Bill felt the world around him grow still. In that moment, there was only her—his partner, his equal, the woman with whom he would share every chapter of his life. When they spoke their vows, their words were not elaborate, but they carried the weight of truth and promise.

"I will walk with you," Bill whispered, his hands cradling hers, "through every season, through every unknown. As long as I have breath, I will love you."

Jane's voice trembled, but her eyes shone with unwavering certainty. "And I with you, Bill. Wherever your path leads, I will follow."

The chapel erupted into quiet applause as they sealed their vows with a kiss. Their marriage, like their love, was not built on grandeur but on the simple, undeniable truth that they belonged together.

Their first home was a small cottage just outside of town, where the scent of fresh parchment and pressed flowers filled the rooms. Jane filled their shelves with books, while Bill filled their garden with herbs and wildflowers, each carefully chosen for their medicinal properties. Their evenings were spent reading by the fire, Bill's head resting against Jane's shoulder as she recited passages from her favorite novels.

Life was not without its struggles. Bill's work often took him into the field, his research demanding long hours of solitude. Yet Jane understood, and she never asked him to be anything other than what he was—a man driven by discovery and wonder. And in return, Bill cherished every moment with her, never taking for granted the love they had built.

One evening, as they sat on their porch watching the stars, Bill reached for Jane's hand. "One day," he mused, "we'll build that cabin in the mountains. A place where the world slows down, where we can sit and watch the sky without distraction."

Jane squeezed his hand. "And we will fill it with books," she said, smiling. "And laughter. And memories."

Bill turned to her, his heart full. "Then it will be home."

And so, their journey together continued, not as an ending, but as the beginning of a life filled with quiet joy, endless curiosity, and a love as steadfast as the stars above.

CHAPTER 6

A HOME IN THE MOUNTAINS

Years passed, and Bill and Jane's dream of a mountain retreat became a reality. In 1922, they settled into a cabin perched on the eastern edge of the Continental Divide, a place where the air was crisp and the mountains stretched endlessly toward the horizon. The cabin, nestled among towering pines, stood three miles by trail from a small town where a school and an orphanage lay at its heart. It was a place of quiet solitude, yet rich with the rhythms of community life.

Jane embraced their new home with the same devotion she had given to every chapter of their life together. She arranged their bookshelves with the care of a curator, ensuring that literature, science, and faith had their place among the worn wooden walls. The scent of drying herbs often mingled with the crisp mountain air as Bill tended to the small garden outside, cultivating plants both medicinal and culinary.

It was during their first year in the mountains that two

new companions entered their lives. Rocky, a sturdy bay horse with a steady gait and an unshakable loyalty to Bill, arrived first. He had been a gift from a local farmer who admired Bill's dedication to his work. Not long after, a golden retriever pup named Champ found his way to their doorstep, a bundle of boundless energy and affection. It was Jane who named him, laughing as the little dog bounded through the grass, his tail wagging with an enthusiasm that never waned.

"This is home," Jane whispered one evening as she stood on the porch, watching the sun dip below the mountains. The golden light bathed the valley in warmth, and Bill, standing beside her, felt the truth of her words settle deep within him.

The small town below became a part of their lives in unexpected ways. Bill, now known simply as "Doc" to the locals, was sought after for his knowledge of plants and natural remedies. The schoolteacher, a kind and bright-eyed woman named Somer, often invited him to speak to her students about the wonders of the natural world. The orphanage, nestled just beyond the town, became another place where Jane and Bill found purpose, reading to the children and offering what care and wisdom they could.

Though they had no children of their own, their days were filled with the laughter and voices of the young ones who came up the trail, eager to learn from Bill's teachings or simply to visit Jane, who always had warm biscuits and a story ready to share.

Evenings at the cabin were moments of peace. Bill would sit on the porch, his pipe in hand, watching the stars flicker to life one by one. The Brown Mountain Lights, those mysterious glows that had puzzled and fascinated travelers for generations, often appeared in the distance, shimmering just beyond the gorge. He would watch them in silence, Jane by his side, Rocky resting nearby, and Champ curled at their feet.

"We've built a good life here," Jane murmured one night, leaning into Bill's shoulder. "A place of learning, of quiet, of love."

Bill pressed a kiss to the top of her head. "A place where we belong."

And with the mountains standing guard and the stars shining above, their home became not just a dwelling, but a sanctuary—a place where knowledge, faith, and love intertwined, creating a legacy that would endure long after they were gone.

Chapter 7

Beneath the Endless Sky

Bill often sat on the front porch of their cabin, a worn pipe in hand, watching the heavens unfold their nightly wonders. The stars, distant yet ever-present, stretched endlessly over the peaks, their celestial dance uninterrupted by time or place. The Brown Mountain Lights flickered like spirits just beyond the gorge, a mystery Bill never tired of contemplating. The vastness of the sky made him feel both infinitesimal and infinite at once, a humble observer of creation's grandeur.

Jane often sat beside him, wrapped in a shawl, her head resting lightly on his shoulder. "Do you ever wonder," she mused one evening, "if the stars remember the people who look up at them? If they carry our stories?"

Bill smiled, squeezing her hand. "I think they do, Jane. I think they hold everything—the past, the present, and all the things we haven't yet dreamed of."

The mountain nights were cold, but their quiet companionship was warm. The glow from the lantern inside the cabin cast a golden light onto the porch, creating a world that felt separate from time itself. Life was measured not in days or years, but in moments like these—watching the heavens, feeling the earth beneath them, and knowing they belonged to each other and to this place.

But time, however gently it passes, does not stop.

Chapter 8

The Silent Winter

The fever came in early winter, when the first heavy snow blanketed the mountains. At first, Jane dismissed it as a passing chill. She wrapped herself in layers, kept warm by the fire, and assured Bill that she would be well by morning. But morning came, and the fever only deepened, stealing the color from her cheeks and the strength from her body.

Bill did everything he could. He brewed teas from the herbs she had taught him to gather, pressed cool cloths to her forehead, whispered reassurances into the night. Champ lay at her bedside, whimpering softly, as if he, too, understood the weight of the moment. Rocky paced outside, restless and uncertain, sensing the shift in the air.

Days passed, and Jane's strength waned. She woke in fevered dreams, speaking in half-formed thoughts of their life together—of the cabin, the books, the children at the orphanage, the stars above. Bill held her through it all, his heart clinging to every breath she took.

One evening, as the fire crackled softly in the hearth, Jane reached for his hand. Her grip was weak but steady, her hazel eyes searching his face. "Bill," she whispered, "promise me... you'll keep watching the stars."

His throat tightened. "Always," he said, pressing her fingers to his lips. "Always."

She smiled, a fragile thing, but full of love. And as the snow fell outside, blanketing the world in quiet, Jane slipped away, carried into the same endless sky they had spent their lives admiring together.

Bill sat beside her for a long time, his fingers entwined with hers, as the fire slowly dimmed. Rocky lowered his head, a sorrowful stillness settling over him. Champ let out a quiet whine, curling closer to the bed as if hoping to keep Jane's warmth beside them just a little longer.

Outside, the stars continued their slow and silent waltz, bearing witness to a love that even time could not diminish.

Chapter 9

The Weight of Silence

The days after Jane's passing were hollow and stretched long into the cold silence of the mountains. Bill could not move from the chair by the hearth where she had last held his hand. The fire had burned down to embers, its warmth fading just as the warmth of her presence had. The cabin, once filled with her laughter and the rustling of book pages, now felt like an empty shell, a house that had lost its soul.

Rocky stood near the doorway, shifting uneasily, as if waiting for Jane to return. Champ lay curled beside Bill's feet, letting out small, mournful sighs, sensing the depth of his master's grief. The world outside went on—snow melted, the wind carried whispers of spring, but inside, Bill remained frozen in place, unable to summon the will to rise.

He tried, on occasion, to step outside, to take up the simple tasks that had once filled his days. But every movement felt wrong without Jane beside him. The kitchen, where she once made tea, seemed foreign to him. The bookshelves, lined with stories they had shared, were too painful to touch. Even the stars, those silent companions he had always turned to, seemed distant now, their beauty muted by sorrow.

The town sent visitors, kind-hearted folk who brought food and soft words of comfort. Somer came from the schoolhouse, placing a gentle hand on his shoulder, offering quiet companionship when words would not do. The children from the orphanage sent hand-drawn pictures of the mountains and the stars, hoping to coax a smile from the man who had once told them stories about both. But Bill could only nod, his voice lost somewhere in the void Jane had left behind.

One evening, long after the last visitor had gone and the cabin had settled into its familiar emptiness, Bill finally rose from his chair. The weight of grief pressed against him, heavy and relentless, but he forced himself to move. He stepped onto the porch where Jane had once sat beside him, wrapped in her shawl, her eyes full of wonder at the night sky. He looked up, and for the first time since she had gone, he whispered her name.

The stars did not answer, but they shone—steady, unwavering, eternal. And Bill, weary and broken, let himself weep beneath them.

CHAPTER 10

CARRYING ON

The days stretched into years, and though grief never fully loosened its hold, Bill learned to live with it. So now it was Bill, Rocky, and Champ keeping house, the three of them bound by unspoken understanding. Rocky, ever steady, carried Bill on long rides through the hills when the cabin walls felt too confining. Champ, full of boundless energy, remained a source of quiet comfort, always at Bill's side, always watchful.

From time to time, Bill would ride down the trail to the small town, visiting the school where Somer still taught. The children, eager and full of life, greeted him as "Doc," as they always had. He spoke to them about the plants of the mountains, their healing properties, and the way nature provided answers if one only knew how to listen.

Sundays brought him to the small church, where he sat in the back pew, nodding at familiar faces, feeling the warmth of shared faith even in his solitude. He never spoke much, but his presence alone was enough for those who had come to respect and care for him. The villagers still sought his knowledge—an old woman with aching joints, a farmer with a sick calf, a mother worried over her child's cough. Bill did what he could, offering remedies passed down through time, his hands steady even when his heart ached.

Then came the letter. It arrived on a gray morning, the ink smudged slightly by dampness. Aunt Maggie had passed. Bill sat on the porch with the letter in his lap, staring out at the mist rolling over the hills. He had not seen her in years, but her voice, sharp and wise, still lived in his mind. It was she who had shaped him, who had taught him the balance of discipline and wonder. And now she, too, was gone.

For a long while, he said nothing. Champ nudged his leg, as if sensing the weight of memory. Bill let out a slow breath and finally stood, walking inside to pull one of her old books from the shelf. He traced his fingers over the pages she had once turned, the words she had once read aloud to him.

He closed his eyes. "Thank you, Aunt Maggie."

Then, with Rocky waiting at the fence and Champ at his heels, Bill saddled up and rode toward town, toward the school, toward life that still remained.

CHAPTER 11

THE SCHOLAR OF THE MOUNTAINS

Bill had always been more than just a healer to the townsfolk—he was a man of discovery, of curiosity that never waned. From time to time, he would stumble upon something remarkable—an unusual herb growing in the shaded crevices of the gorge, a fossil embedded in the rocky riverbanks, a peculiar reaction between plants and soil that defied conventional knowledge. These moments, these quiet discoveries, would send him back to his desk, where he would carefully document his findings in meticulous handwriting, filling pages upon pages of scholarly journals. His observations, bound in leather notebooks, often found their way into scientific publications, though Bill never sought fame or recognition.

His passion for knowledge extended beyond his own studies. He had taken to teaching Somer, the schoolteacher, about herbal medicines. She was eager to learn, listening intently as Bill explained the uses of mountain mint for fevers or the way black cohosh eased pain.

"Nature gives us everything we need," he told her one afternoon, handing her a bundle of dried herbs. "If we know how to listen."

She nodded, tucking the herbs into her satchel. "Then teach me how to listen."

Their lessons expanded into something greater—classes for the children at the school. Bill, who had once stood before university students in lecture halls, now found himself kneeling in the dirt, showing wide-eyed children how to identify plants by their scent and shape. He led them into the woods, where he taught them how to recognize healing roots and poisonous leaves, how to read the land as if it were a book written in green and stone.

One bright autumn afternoon, he knelt beside a group of students who were gathered around a cluster of wild mushrooms. "These," he said, pointing to the delicate caps, "are safe. But these—" he gestured to another patch, "—can make you terribly ill. One mistake, and you could be in real trouble."

A boy raised his hand. "How do you know which is which?"

Bill smiled. "By paying attention. By knowing their shape, their color, even their smell. It's all about learning the language of nature."

The children hung on to his every word, and in those moments, Bill felt something stir within him—a sense of purpose, a reason to keep moving forward. He was not just a man who had lost; he was a man who still had so much to give.

Even as the years passed, as his hair grayed and his hands grew slower, Bill continued to teach, to write, to share what he had learned with anyone willing to listen. And at night, as he sat on his porch, watching the stars wheel overhead, he knew that Jane would have been proud of him. Proud that he had not let grief consume him. Proud that he had kept going, one discovery, one lesson, one shared moment at a time.

CHAPTER 12

WISDOM OF THE EARTH

Bill's days in the mountains had become a quiet rhythm of study, teaching, and tending to the land. His grief had not left him, but it had softened into something bearable, something that lived within him like the whisper of wind through the trees. And though the years had made his steps slower and his hands more lined, his mind remained as sharp as ever, always searching for new mysteries in the world around him.

From time to time, Bill would make biological discoveries that stirred his old academic instincts. He still wrote, filling his leather-bound journals with notes on herbal reactions, the behavior of mountain flora, and the healing properties of plants that had yet to be studied in depth. Some of these findings made their way into scientific journals, though Bill sought no acclaim. It was enough to know that his work might help someone, somewhere, long after he was gone.

His knowledge was not confined to his own notebooks.

He had taken Somer under his wing, passing on what he knew about medicinal plants and their uses. She was a quick learner, eager and thoughtful, often asking questions that even Bill had to pause and consider.

One afternoon, as they walked through a sun-dappled grove near the school, Bill knelt beside a cluster of blue cohosh. He carefully plucked a leaf and handed it to her.

"This one," he said, "helps with fever and pain. But mix it wrong, and it can do more harm than good."

Somer turned the leaf over in her fingers, studying it. "How do you know how much to use?"

Bill smiled. "You listen. To the plant, to the body, to the land. Nature has a balance, and if you respect it, it will tell you what you need to know."

She nodded, tucking the leaf into her satchel. "I want to learn everything you know."

"Then you will," Bill said simply.

His teachings extended beyond Somer. The children at the school had taken to calling him "Professor Bill," though he always waved them off with a chuckle. He led them on nature walks through the hills, showing them how to recognize different plants, teaching them which ones could be brewed into teas and which should never be touched. Their laughter and questions reminded him of his younger self, wandering the lowlands with a notebook in hand, hungry for knowledge.

One afternoon, a young boy named Daniel tugged on Bill's sleeve as they examined a patch of wild mushrooms.

"Professor Bill, how do you know if something is good or bad?" the boy asked, pointing at the fungi.

Bill chuckled. "That's a question bigger than mushrooms, Daniel." He knelt down and pointed at two mush-rooms, nearly identical. "This one here? Harmless. But this one?" He tapped the other with a finger. "Poison. They look alike, don't they?"

Daniel nodded.

Bill sat back. "That's why we learn, why we observe. Because things aren't always what they seem at first glance. Whether it's plants, people, or choices, you have to take the time to understand before you decide what's good or bad."

The boy considered this for a long moment before nodding solemnly. Bill smiled, ruffling his hair before standing.

These moments, these quiet lessons, became the fabric of Bill's days. He no longer stood in grand lecture halls or wrote academic papers read by scholars, but here, among the trees and the eager minds of the next generation, he had found something even greater—a legacy that would outlive him, rooted in the mountains he called home.

CHAPTER 13

THE FEVER STRIKES

The evening air had been still, carrying only the faint hum of insects and the distant hoot of an owl. Bill had been sitting on his porch, watching the last embers of sunset fade behind the mountains when Champ let out a low, uneasy growl. Rocky shifted in the pasture, ears flicking toward the valley below. Something was wrong.

In town, lanterns flickered in windows where they shouldn't have. People moved in hurried steps through the streets, whispering with urgency. It wasn't until Somer arrived at Bill's cabin, her face pale and drawn, that he realized the extent of what had happened.

"It's the well," she gasped, barely pausing to catch her breath. "The children—they're sick. Almost all of them."

Bill felt his heart tighten. "Tell me everything."

She swallowed hard. "The community well—there was a possum. It must have been sick. It fell in. We found it this morning, but by then—" She shook her head. "The children drank the water before anyone knew."

Bill grabbed his satchel and rifle, not for hunting, but for protection—against what, he wasn't yet sure. The moment they reached town, the severity of the situation became clear. The schoolhouse had been turned into a makeshift infirmary. Children lay on cots, their small bodies burning with fever, their breath shallow and labored. Some whimpered, others moaned in their fevered sleep. Mothers and fathers stood helplessly at their sides, pressing damp cloths to their foreheads, praying for relief.

Bill knelt beside the first child, a boy no older than eight. His skin was slick with sweat, his breathing ragged. Bill pressed a hand to his forehead—burning hot. He moved from child to child, each one the same, all gripped by the fever. He exchanged glances with Somer, who was doing her best to comfort the younger ones.

"How long since the first symptoms?" Bill asked, rolling up his sleeves.

"Last night," Somer said. "It started with stomach pain, then fever. By morning, more than half the school was sick."

Bill's mind raced. "Rabies?" He murmured. No, that wasn't right. This wasn't the rapid decline he'd seen in rabid animals. But if the possum had been diseased, if the well had been contaminated, there was no telling what was attacking the children's bodies.

He turned to the desperate parents. "We need fresh water. Boil everything. No one touches that well." His voice was firm, unwavering, even as panic tightened its grip on the room.

A man in the doorway shifted uneasily. "Doc," he said. "We've sent for help, but it'll take days. Asheville's too far, and we ain't got a doctor close enough to help."

Bill took a slow breath, steadying himself. He had no time for fear. He had to think. "Then we do what we can," he said. "And we pray it's enough."

He met Somer's gaze. "We start now."

As the night deepened, the battle for the children's lives began.

CHAPTER 14

A PRAYER FOR LIGHT

The fever did not break. The night was heavy with worry, the air thick with the scent of damp cloths and burning candles. Somer had come up the trail to Bill's cabin, her breath ragged, her hands trembling.

"They're getting worse," she said. "Some of them aren't waking up."

Bill saddled Rocky without a word and rode into town, Champ running beside him. The schoolhouse was silent save for the labored breathing of the sick, the occasional muffled sob of a parent, the creaking floorboards beneath Bill's boots.

He examined each child, looking for signs—anything that might tell him what they were fighting. He had them spit into a Petri dish, sealing it carefully, hands steady despite the weight of uncertainty pressing on his heart. The sample would be sent to Winston-Salem by morning, but that answer would take time, and time was something they didn't have. The fevers were climbing. The prayers were growing desperate.

That night, Bill knelt beside his bed, his hands clasped so tightly that his knuckles turned white. He was not a man prone to asking for miracles, but as he looked out at the stars —those same stars he had shared with Jane—he found himself speaking aloud.

"Lord," he whispered, his voice breaking, "I don't know what to do. These children, this town—they need something greater than me. I have done all I can, and still, I am lost. If ever I have needed Your guidance, it is now."

Silence answered him, but it was not empty. The wind stirred outside, rustling the leaves as if whispering back to him. The memory of Jane's voice echoed in his mind, her words from years before: *Do you ever wonder if the stars remember the people who look up at them?*

Bill took a slow breath, steadying himself. The weight of grief, of helplessness, had not lifted, but something settled within him—a sense that he was not alone in this fight.

He rose, his resolve firm. God had not spoken in a voice of thunder or parted the heavens, but He had reminded Bill of something vital: he was not without purpose. There was still work to do, and he would see it done.

Morning came, and Bill stepped out onto the porch, ready to face whatever lay ahead. He would not stop. Not now. Not ever. The battle was far from over, but faith had found its way into the fight.

Chapter 15

The Answer in the Dark

Sleep did not come easily to Bill that night. Exhaustion weighed heavy on his body, but his mind refused to rest. Each time he closed his eyes, the images of the fevered children haunted him—their flushed faces, their weak cries, the fear in their parents' eyes. The weight of responsibility pressed against his chest, suffocating and relentless.

The cabin was dark save for the embers smoldering in the fireplace. Outside, the wind whispered through the trees, carrying with it the distant call of a night bird. Rocky shifted in the barn, his hooves stirring the straw. Champ lay curled at the foot of Bill's bed, ears twitching in restless sleep.

Then, just as he drifted into uneasy slumber, a feeling stirred within him—something insistent, something unshakable. He woke with a start, his heart pounding in his chest. The air in the cabin felt different, thick with an urgency he couldn't explain. He sat up, rubbing the sleep from his eyes, and felt the pull—the unshakable sense that he needed to move, to go outside.

Barefoot and still drowsy, Bill pulled his coat over his nightshirt and stepped onto the porch. The cold bit at his skin, but he barely noticed. Above him, the stars were impossibly bright, scattered like jewels across the black velvet sky. He took a deep breath, steadying himself, and then he prayed.

"Lord," he murmured, his breath curling into the night air. "If there's something I haven't seen, show me. If there's something I've missed, lead me to it."

The wind stirred, rustling the trees, and Bill felt it then—a whisper of an idea, sudden and clear. His mind latched onto it, heart pounding faster as realization struck. The well. The water. The sickness.

His boots crunched against the frost-covered ground as he strode toward the town's well. Champ, sensing his urgency, trotted beside him. The night was quiet, save for the rustling of leaves and the occasional hoot of an owl.

As he neared the well, the scent hit him first—an acrid, sickly-sweet smell that didn't belong. His stomach twisted. He lifted the lantern higher and peered into the depths.

There, caught against the stone, half-submerged in the murky water, was the answer. A possum, bloated and lifeless, its fur matted, its body twisted unnaturally.

Bill's breath caught in his throat. "Dear God…"

He stepped back, composing himself. He knew, now, what had poisoned the children. The realization filled him with both relief and dread. Relief, because he had found the cause. Dread, because time was running out.

Without wasting a second, he hurried back toward town. The general store would still be dark at this hour, but that didn't matter. Bill pounded on the door until a light flickered inside. A moment later, the shopkeeper, a grizzled man named Hank, opened the door, his eyes bleary with sleep.

"Bill?" he grunted. "What in the blazes—?"

"I need you to send a telegram," Bill said breathlessly. "Right now. To Winston-Salem. The hospital."

Hank blinked, rubbing his eyes. "You found something?"

Bill nodded. "It's the well, Hank. A rabid possum got in. We need confirmation, but I'm almost certain that's what's poisoning the children."

Hank swore under his breath but didn't argue. He knew Bill well enough to trust him. "Alright," he said, stepping aside. "Let's send the message."

By the time the first light of dawn stretched over the mountains, the telegram was on its way. Bill stood outside the store, watching the sky shift from indigo to soft pink, exhaustion weighing heavy on his limbs. But for the first time in days, he felt something close to hope.

Now, all they could do was wait for an answer.

CHAPTER 16

A RACE AGAINST TIME

The schoolhouse had become a battlefield, and Bill and Somer were fighting against an enemy they could not see. The fevered children lay sprawled on cots, their small bodies burning with sickness. Some moaned in their restless sleep, others were too weak to move. Parents hovered beside them, their faces etched with exhaustion and fear. The air inside was thick with the scent of damp cloths and desperation.

Bill wiped the sweat from his brow, his hands trembling from exhaustion. He and Somer had done everything they could—cool compresses, herbal tinctures, makeshift hydration solutions—but it was not enough. The children needed IVs, medicines he did not have, and proper care that only trained doctors could provide.

"The telegram's sent," Hank had told him earlier that morning. "The doctors from Asheville are coming. But it'll take three days."

Three days. Bill had nodded grimly, but inside, dread

clawed at him. Three days was too long for some of these children. He saw it in their sunken cheeks, in the way their chests rattled with every breath. Time was slipping through his fingers like sand.

Somer knelt beside one of the younger boys, dabbing his forehead with a cool cloth. "Bill," she said softly, her voice thick with worry. "He's getting worse."

Bill crouched beside her, pressing his fingers to the boy's wrist. His pulse was faint, fluttering like a moth against glass. He met Somer's eyes, and for the first time, he saw his own fear reflected in them.

"We need to do more," she whispered.

Bill exhaled slowly. "We need a miracle."

Outside, the sky had darkened, clouds rolling in over the mountains like great waves of ink. A storm was coming. The air was heavy, thick with the promise of rain, but even that would not be enough to wash away the sickness that gripped the town.

Just then, a commotion at the door made Bill look up. A man stumbled in, panting heavily. It was Henry Dawson, a farmer from the outskirts of town. "Doc," he wheezed, bracing himself against the doorframe. "You gotta come. My boy—he just took a turn. It's bad."

Bill hesitated. Leaving the schoolhouse, even for a short time, meant taking a risk. But Henry's face was pale with terror, and Bill knew he could not ignore it.

Somer touched his arm. "Go," she said. "I'll stay here. I'll do what I can."

Bill gave her a firm nod before grabbing his satchel. He strode out into the darkening evening, Rocky already saddled and waiting. He mounted quickly, and Champ, sensing the urgency, ran alongside them as they raced toward the Dawson farm.

Lightning flickered in the distance, illuminating the landscape in sharp bursts. The wind howled through the trees as they rode, the weight of responsibility pressing down on Bill's chest. He could not let another child slip away.

When they arrived at the farmhouse, Henry's wife was waiting at the door, her hands clasped in silent prayer. "He's inside," she whispered, her eyes brimming with unshed tears.

Bill stepped into the dimly lit room and was immediately met with the sound of labored breathing. The boy, no older than ten, lay sprawled on the bed, his body wracked with fever, his lips cracked and dry.

Bill swallowed the lump in his throat and got to work. He would not stop. Not until the doctors arrived. Not until he had done everything in his power to save them.

And still, in the back of his mind, he prayed—prayed for strength, for guidance, for the storm outside to pass and the storm within these children to break before it was too late.

CHAPTER 17

A DIVINE VISITOR

That night, after tending to the Dawson boy for hours, Bill finally returned to his cabin. Exhaustion pressed against him like a heavy cloak, but sleep did not come easily. His mind churned with worry, each breath of the wind outside carrying whispers of desperation from the town below. The storm had passed, but the fever had not, and the children still lay weak and suffering.

Unable to rest, Bill knelt beside his bed and bowed his head. His voice, hoarse from fatigue, rose in a quiet, fervent prayer. "Lord, I've done all I can. I've given every remedy I know, I've sent for help, but it may not come in time. These little ones—they need more than I can give. Show me the way."

Hours later, in the deep stillness of the night, Champ stirred at the foot of the bed, letting out a low whimper. Bill, groggy and disoriented, opened his eyes. The cabin, usually dim in the moonlight, was awash in an ethereal glow. A presence filled the room—not frightening, but powerful, vast yet gentle.

At the foot of his bed stood a figure unlike any Bill had ever seen. Cloaked in flowing robes of silver and gold, the being's face shone with an otherworldly light, eyes deep and knowing. A profound peace settled over Bill as he gazed upon the visitor, and without needing to be told, he understood.

"Archangel Raphael," Bill whispered, his breath catching.

The being inclined his head, radiating warmth and wisdom. "You have called for guidance, and so I have come." The voice was rich and steady, neither loud nor soft, but resounding in the very marrow of Bill's bones. "The fever that plagues your town is curable, but you must act swiftly."

Bill swallowed hard, forcing himself to his feet. "Tell me what I need to do."

Raphael extended a luminous hand, and suddenly Bill saw images flashing through his mind—visions of plants growing deep within the gorge, herbs he had studied but never considered for fever. He saw himself gathering them, boiling them into a tonic, administering it to the children. Hope surged within him.

"But how do I know it will work?" Bill asked, still grasping at reason.

The angel's gaze softened. "You have always trusted the wisdom of the land. Trust it now. You were given this knowledge for a reason."

The glow in the room slowly faded, and as it did, Bill felt warmth fill his chest, an energy he had not known in years.

When the light was gone, he was left alone in the quiet of his cabin, the weight of doubt replaced with resolve.

Champ let out a low sigh, settling back into sleep. Bill stood, already reaching for his satchel. He had no time to waste. The answer had been given—now it was up to him to act before it was too late.

CHAPTER 18

THE HEALING BEGINS

Bill did not hesitate. He grabbed his satchel and strode into the night, the angel's words still ringing in his ears. The air was cool, the mountains shrouded in a thick mist, but he moved with purpose, driven by the urgency of the message he had received. The children were running out of time, and he had been given the tools to save them.

He reached the well just as the first light of dawn began to creep over the horizon. The town was still quiet, the only sounds the distant rustling of leaves and the gentle hum of waking birds. He knelt beside the well, peering down into the dark water below. This was the source of the illness, the poisoned lifeline of the village.

Raphael's instructions were clear. Bill reached into his satchel, pulling out a small vial filled with iodine and salt—the very elements needed to cleanse the well. He poured it in slowly, watching as the water absorbed the mixture. Then, he took hold of the pump handle and began to work.

One. Two. Three times, he pumped, sending the tainted

water cascading over the ground. He could hear footsteps approaching—Somer, Hank, and a few of the townspeople, their faces drawn with exhaustion and worry.

"What are you doing, Bill?" Somer asked, her voice barely above a whisper.

"Cleaning the well," he said, his hands gripping the pump with steady determination. "It has to be done seven times. That's what I was told."

Somer's brow furrowed. "Told by who?"

Bill hesitated for only a moment before looking at her. "An angel."

She blinked, uncertainty flickering in her eyes, but she did not question him. Instead, she reached for the pump. "Then let's finish it."

Together, they worked until the seventh and final pumping was done. The water ran clean and clear, the sickly scent of decay finally gone. Bill wiped the sweat from his brow and turned to the crowd that had gathered.

"This water is safe now," he said. "No one is to drink from it until it settles, but it will no longer make anyone sick."

A murmur ran through the people, a mixture of relief and skepticism. But there was no time to debate. The children still burned with fever, and there was one more task left to complete.

Bill reached into his pocket, feeling the smooth glass of the vial Raphael had given him. It was small, impossibly so, barely the size of his thumb. Doubt threatened to creep in. Would this be enough? Could something so small cure an entire village?

As if sensing his thoughts, the angel's voice echoed in his

mind. *"Don't you remember the story of the Loaves and Fishes? Jesus sent this for the children and anyone who needs it."*

A shiver ran down Bill's spine. Faith, he reminded himself. He had trusted before—he would trust now.

He turned to Somer and handed her the vial. "Mix this with warm water and give it to the children. A few drops for each one."

Somer took it hesitantly, looking at him. "Will it be enough?"

Bill's voice was steady. "It will."

They moved swiftly, returning to the schoolhouse where the children lay. Somer worked quickly, diluting the liquid and administering it to the small, parched mouths of the sick. Parents watched with wide, desperate eyes, clinging to hope.

The waiting was the hardest part. Bill sat beside one of the younger children, pressing a damp cloth to her forehead. He prayed, not just for her, but for all of them. Time slowed, stretching unbearably. Then, as the first rays of morning light seeped through the windows, a miracle unfolded.

One by one, the children's breathing grew steadier. Their fevers, once raging, began to break. The harsh, painful coughs softened. A mother gasped as her son's eyes fluttered open, his gaze no longer clouded with fever but filled with recognition. A little girl sat up, weak but alert, reaching for her mother's hand.

Tears of relief filled the room. Parents embraced their children, whispering prayers of thanks. Somer pressed a shaking hand to her lips, looking at Bill with something between awe and gratitude.

He exhaled, his own eyes burning with unshed tears. It had worked. God had answered.

Outside, the sun rose higher over the mountains, bathing the town in golden light. The storm had passed. The fever had lifted. And in that moment, Bill knew that he had witnessed something far greater than himself—a miracle born not just of medicine, but of faith.

CHAPTER 19

———————

THE MIDNIGHT RIDE

The night was silent, the world wrapped in a cloak of darkness, save for the glow of Bill's oil lantern. He saddled Rocky with practiced hands, his movements steady despite the weight of exhaustion pressing upon him. Champ, ever faithful, stood at attention, ears pricked forward as if he, too, understood the urgency of the night's mission.

Bill took a deep breath and laid the reins down on Rocky's neck. The horse knew the trail well, having traveled it many times before. With a quiet nudge of his heel, Bill set off down the winding path, the oil lantern casting long flickering shadows against the trees. Champ trotted ahead, leading the way as he always did, his golden coat barely visible in the dim light.

The mountain air was cold, crisp with the lingering dampness of the passing storm. Bill's breath curled in the air, mixing with the rhythmic sound of Rocky's hooves against the dirt path. The ride to the orphanage felt longer in the night, the silence stretching between each gust of wind. But Bill was resolute. He had seen the miracle unfold at the schoolhouse, had watched the fevered children open their eyes once more. Now, there were more who needed saving.

The orphanage was quiet when Bill arrived. The building loomed in the soft glow of his lantern, its windows dark, its occupants lost in uneasy sleep. Bill dismounted, his boots crunching against the damp earth, and strode to the door. He rapped firmly, not wanting to startle the sleeping children, but enough to wake the caretaker inside.

A few moments later, a weary-looking woman cracked open the door, her expression shifting from surprise to relief when she saw Bill standing there. "Bill?" she whispered. "What is it?"

"No time to explain," he said gently but firmly. "I have something that will help."

The woman hesitated only a moment before stepping aside, motioning him in. Inside, the air was thick with warmth, but there was an underlying tension, the unmistakable presence of worry that had settled over the orphanage like a heavy quilt.

Bill moved from bed to bed, gently shaking each child awake. Their faces, still flushed from lingering fever, turned toward him with sleepy confusion. He spoke to them in a soft, reassuring tone, offering each a sip from the small vial the angel had given him.

"Just a little," he murmured to a boy who blinked up at him groggily. "It'll help, I promise."

One by one, he administered the liquid, watching as their tense little bodies relaxed, their breathing becoming steadier. As he worked, the caretaker gathered the staff and the few parents who had remained overnight.

"Everyone must take a sip," Bill said, holding the vial out. "This isn't just for the children—it's for anyone who needs it."

The adults hesitated, staring at the vial in his hand. "What is it?" one man asked.

Bill's fingers tightened around the small glass bottle. "It's a gift," he said simply. "A blessing."

The first parent stepped forward, a mother wrapped in a wool shawl, her face pale with worry. She took the vial, tipped a drop onto her tongue, and then her eyes widened slightly. "It's sweet," she murmured, surprised. "Like honey."

The others followed, one by one, each taking a sip, their expressions shifting from doubt to quiet wonder. Whatever was in that vial, it was unlike anything they had ever tasted.

Bill let out a slow breath, feeling the weight of the night pressing down on him. He had done all he could. Now, it was in God's hands.

As he stepped back out into the cold night air, the wind rustled through the trees, carrying with it a feeling of peace he hadn't known in years. He mounted Rocky once more, Champ falling into step beside them, and rode back into the night, the oil lantern swaying gently with each step.

The sickness would soon be gone. The fever would break. And as Bill rode home beneath the watchful gaze of the stars, he whispered a quiet prayer of thanks, knowing deep in his soul that the miracle was not just in the cure, but in the faith that had carried them through.

Chapter 20

A Prayer of Gratitude

Dawn broke over the mountains with a golden glow, the mist rising from the valleys like a breath exhaled by the land itself. The town had been holding its breath for days, waiting, praying, hoping. Now, as morning light filtered through the trees, a change had come—one that was felt in the very air.

The fever had broken.

Mothers pressed cool hands to their children's foreheads and found only warmth, not the fire that had burned them before. Fathers embraced one another, their relief unspoken but heavy in the way they clasped hands. The schoolhouse and orphanage, once hushed with sickness and whispered prayers, were now alive with the soft sounds of waking children, their voices no longer weak but growing strong.

Bill stood near the well, his hands braced on the worn wooden pump, exhaustion settled deep into his bones. He had barely slept in days, and yet, as he looked around at the people gathering, the relief and joy in their eyes, he felt a strength that did not come from rest, but from purpose.

Someone began to hum a hymn—soft at first, then joined by another voice, and another. Soon, the entire community stood together, their voices rising in unison as they sang a song of thanksgiving. The sound carried across the valley, filling the morning air with praise.

"Thank you, Jesus," a woman whispered, her hands clasped over her heart.

A father knelt beside his son, pressing his forehead to the child's and murmuring, "Thank you, Lord. Thank you."

Somer wiped at her eyes, her voice unsteady but full of conviction. "We should gather," she said, turning to Bill. "We should pray together."

Word spread quickly, and soon, the people of the town gathered outside the small church. The doors were flung open, and despite the early hour, the pews filled with men, women, and children—some still weak from their sickness, but all of them whole. Bill hesitated at the entrance, but Somer gently took his arm and led him inside.

The preacher, an elderly man with a voice like rolling thunder, stepped to the pulpit, his eyes glistening with emotion. He raised his hands over the congregation, and silence fell.

"This town has seen a miracle," he said, his voice steady. "We have witnessed the power of faith, the grace of healing, the hand of God working through those among us. Let us give thanks."

Heads bowed, hands clasped, voices lifted.

"Thank you, Jesus."

The words rippled through the church, not just from

the preacher, but from every heart present. Some wept, some smiled through their tears, some simply sat in silence, feeling the presence of something greater than themselves.

As the prayer came to an end, Bill felt a warmth settle in his chest. Not just relief, not just gratitude, but peace. He had spent so long searching—for answers in science, for healing in the land, for purpose in his work. But here, now, he understood.

Faith and knowledge were not at odds. They had never been. They were two paths leading to the same truth, woven together like the roots of the trees that surrounded them. He had done what he could, and when that was not enough, he had been given a sign. He had trusted, and he had been answered.

As the congregation slowly rose, lingering in quiet conversation and embraces, Bill turned to Somer. She smiled at him, a silent acknowledgment passing between them.

"You did good, Doc," she said softly.

Bill exhaled, a small smile tugging at the corners of his mouth. "We all did."

Outside, the morning sun was bright, the sky clear, the mountains standing tall and steady as they always had. The town had endured. The people had endured. And in their hearts, they knew—they had been blessed.

And so, as the town moved forward, forever changed by what they had witnessed, their voices remained strong in gratitude: *Thank you, Jesus.*

CHAPTER 21

THE ANGEL'S FAREWELL

Bill stayed at the schoolhouse for the rest of the night and into midday, watching over the children with quiet vigilance. As the hours passed, the fever that had once burned so fiercely began to fade. One by one, the children stirred, their eyes losing the dull haze of sickness and filling once more with life. Their small voices, weak but growing stronger, whispered of hunger. It was the most welcome sound Bill had heard in days.

By noon, the schoolhouse was alive again. Mothers brought broth and fresh bread, spooning it carefully to their recovering little ones. Fathers shook Bill's hand, their grips firm with gratitude. The relief in the air was thick, almost tangible, as laughter—soft and hesitant at first—began to weave through the space that had been so quiet with worry only hours before.

Somer placed a hand on Bill's shoulder. "It's over," she said, her voice filled with emotion. "They're going to be alright."

Bill let out a long breath, as if finally releasing the weight of the past few days. He nodded, but his heart still felt the tremors of exhaustion. He had given everything he had, and now, the town no longer needed him for this fight. It was time to go home.

As evening stretched across the valley, Bill saddled Rocky and began the slow ride back to his cabin. Champ ran ahead, his golden coat catching the last light of the sun. The trail was familiar, but tonight, it felt different—lighter, quieter, as if the mountains themselves had exhaled in relief.

When he reached the cabin, he unsaddled Rocky, rubbing the horse's neck with an affectionate hand before leading him to the water trough. The rhythmic sound of Rocky drinking was steady, grounding. Champ flopped onto the porch, his tail thumping lazily against the wood.

Bill stepped inside, brewing a fresh cup of coffee, the rich aroma filling the space. He took it outside and settled into his rocking chair, gazing up at the sky. The stars were out in full brilliance, scattered across the heavens like diamonds spilled from a great celestial hand. The air was crisp, and for the first time in days, Bill let himself relax.

Then, as he took a slow sip of his coffee, something caught his eye. A star, brighter than the others, moved across the sky in a smooth, graceful arc. Bill watched as it shot toward the horizon—then, just before it disappeared, it seemed to pause, wobbling its light like a flickering wing.

Bill exhaled slowly, a knowing smile tugging at the corners of his mouth.

The angel was going home.

For a long time, Bill sat there, the warmth of the coffee in his hands and the peace of the night settling over him. He had done what he was meant to do. The town was safe. The children would grow. The mountains would remain.

And somewhere, in the vast expanse of the heavens, Raphael watched over them all.

Chapter 22

The Watcher of the Stars

The days settled into a quiet rhythm once more, but Bill's nights belonged to the sky. His porch had become his television screen, his entertainment the endless panoply of the heavens stretching before him. Out here, on the edge of the mountains, where the sky met the earth in a vast embrace, the stars performed a nightly show just for him.

The nights were crisp, the air humming with the sounds of crickets and the distant call of an owl. Bill would settle into his rocking chair, a warm cup of coffee or a pipe in hand, Champ lying at his feet, and Rocky dozing lazily in the pasture. The universe stretched above him in its infinite display, the constellations wheeling slowly through the blackened sky. He traced them with his eyes, whispering their names as he had since childhood—Orion, Cassiopeia, the Pleiades. He had learned them as a boy, studied them as a man, and now, in his later years, he simply watched them as an old friend watches another, no words needed.

Every now and then, one of them would move—just a flicker, a slight deviation from the predictable waltz of the cosmos. A star-breaking formation, slipping out of line, darting across the heavens in a way that made no sense. It wasn't like a meteor, which streaked fast and burned away. No, these stars danced differently. They paused, shifted, wobbled their wings, as if acknowledging his gaze.

Bill never said a word about it to anyone. What was there to say? Who would believe an old mountain man who claimed the stars didn't always behave? But he knew what he saw. And in the quiet, he would nod, tipping his coffee cup ever so slightly, as if toasting whatever force, whatever presence, might be looking back at him.

"Maybe it's just the wind in my eyes," he muttered to Champ one evening. The dog huffed, shifting his weight but never lifting his head.

Or maybe, just maybe, it wasn't.

The thought didn't scare him. Quite the opposite. It filled him with a strange kind of comfort. A reminder that the world was still full of mysteries, that there were things beyond human understanding, and that perhaps, somewhere out there, something still watched over him.

So Bill kept watching. The nights passed, the stars continued their dance, and every so often—just often enough to keep him wondering—one would move in a way it shouldn't. And Bill would smile to himself, knowing that not all things in this world or the next could be explained.

CHAPTER 23

───────

THE MAN THEY CALLED DOC

Time moved differently in the mountains. Days stretched long and slow, measured not by the ticking of clocks but by the shifting of light over the peaks, the way the mist rolled in the mornings and burned away by noon. Bill had long since stopped marking the years; instead, he counted the seasons, the faces that came and went, the stories that lingered in the wind.

Retirement, if one could call it that, had not slowed him down much. The people in town still came to him, knocking on his door or stopping him on his way to the post office. They called him *Doc* now, though he had never been a doctor in the official sense. He was something else—a healer of sorts, a man who knew the land and its secrets, who could soothe both wounds of the body and those of the heart.

His relationship with the town had deepened over the years. The orphanage remained close to his heart, and he often found himself there, helping where he could. The director, a stern but kind woman named Miss Evelyn Clarke, had grown to trust him like family. "Doc, you've got a way with these children," she told him once, as he sat on the porch carving a whistle for one of the younger boys. "They listen to you."

Bill only smiled. "Maybe because I listen to them first."

The school, too, remained a place where his presence was always welcome. Somer, ever eager to learn, had expanded her lessons to include some of Bill's teachings, weaving in herbal lore and the study of nature alongside the usual arithmetic and history. "You've made these children curious, Doc," she told him after one lesson. "They want to see the world the way you do."

Bill chuckled. "Then they'll never run out of things to learn."

At the post office, old Hank, the postmaster, always had a letter or a package set aside for him—sometimes a journal from a fellow scholar, sometimes a note from a traveler passing through who had heard of the mountain man who knew the stars. "You're famous, Doc," Hank would joke. "Not bad for a fella who never asked for attention."

Even the local sheriff, a quiet but watchful man named Tom Callahan, had come to rely on Bill's wisdom from time to time. "You see things different, Doc," he admitted one evening as they sat outside the general store. "Sometimes I need that kind of thinking."

Bill had only nodded, knowing that sometimes, understanding people and the land was more valuable than enforcing the law.

And always, there was the Gorge. The wild, untamed land that called to him even after all these years. He still took treks through the rocky paths, following trails few dared to walk. There, among the ancient stones and whispering trees, he felt closest to something greater, something vast and eternal. Some nights, he would sit on the edge of a high ridge, gazing into the abyss below as the Brown Mountain Lights flickered in the distance, mysteries as old as time.

His evenings, more often than not, ended on his porch, a warm cup of coffee in hand, Champ curled beside him, Rocky grazing in the distance. The stars above stretched endlessly, silent and watching. And sometimes, just sometimes, one of them would move differently—just enough to remind him that the world still held its wonders, and that perhaps, somewhere out there, something was still watching over him, too.

Bill McBannon was not a young man anymore. But he was still *Doc*, the man who had lived and learned, who had healed and taught, who had loved and lost and kept going. And though his story was nearing its later chapters, he knew —deep in his bones—that it was not over just yet.

CHAPTER 24

A LIFE WELL LIVED

The mountain air was crisp, the stars scattered like a thousand memories across the vast night sky. Bill McBannon rocked gently on his porch, his old hands wrapped around a warm cup of coffee, the steam curling into the cool evening air. Champ lay beside him, his breathing slow and steady, and Rocky stood quietly in the pasture, his dark form barely visible against the starlit backdrop.

Bill's mind wandered, not in confusion, but in quiet reflection. A lifetime stretched behind him, filled with moments that now felt like echoes carried by the wind. He had been a boy once, full of wonder, raised by Aunt Maggie, who had taught him discipline and curiosity in equal measure. He had left home, wide-eyed and eager, stepping into the halls of Wake Forest, where books and knowledge had shaped him into a scholar.

He had loved Jane, his dearest Jane, whose presence still lingered in the quiet corners of his heart. Their years together had been filled with learning, laughter, and the simple joys of a shared life. Her loss had nearly broken him, but he had carried on, finding purpose in the land, in the stars, in the people who needed him.

The children at the school, the orphans who clung to his stories, the villagers who had come to know him as *Doc*—they had become his family, his legacy. He had spent his later years teaching, healing, and wandering the Gorge, the place that had always felt like home. And then there had been the sickness, the long nights, the prayers whispered into the dark. The fever had come, and with it, the test of all he had learned and believed. He had been given a gift, a sign, and he had followed it, trusting in something greater than himself. The angel had come, and the miracle had unfolded.

Now, the town had healed. The children had grown. Somer had taken over much of what he once did, carrying on his teachings, ensuring that his knowledge would not be lost. The sheriff still stopped by to talk. The postmaster still saved letters for him, though fewer arrived these days. The Gorge remained unchanged, ancient and knowing, as if it had always been waiting for him to return to it.

Bill exhaled slowly, setting his cup down on the worn wooden railing of the porch. He gazed up at the sky, the constellations shifting in their eternal dance. And then, as if in quiet confirmation, one star moved—not like a shooting star, not like a meteor, but with intention, with a gentle, knowing wobble, as if it were tipping its wings to him one last time.

Bill smiled, slow and full, feeling the warmth of everything he had ever been and everything he had ever done settle deep within him. His story was not one of great fame or riches, but it was full. Full of love, of purpose, of wonder. A life well lived.

The mountains had watched over him, the stars had guided him, and faith had carried him. And as he leaned back in his chair, the night wrapping itself around him, he knew he had never truly been alone.

He never would be.

The End.

www.ingramcontent.com/pod-product-compliance
Lightning Source LLC
Chambersburg PA
CBHW050806160726
48004CB00002B/728